Little Bo Peep's Missing Sheep

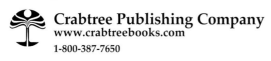

Crabtree Publishing Company
www.crabtreebooks.com
1-800-387-7650

PMB 59051
350 Fifth Ave., 59th Floor,
New York, NY 10118

616 Welland Ave.
St. Catharines, ON
L2M 5V6

Published by Crabtree Publishing in 2013

Series editor: Louise John
Editors: Katie Powell, Kathy Middleton
Notes to adults: Reagan Miller
Cover design: Paul Cherrill
Design: D.R.ink
Consultant: Shirley Bickler
Production coordinator and
    Prepress technician: Margaret Amy Salter
Print coordinator: Katherine Berti

Text © Alan Durant 2009
Illustration © Leah-Ellen Heming 2009

First published in
2009 by Wayland
(A division of Hachette
Children's Books)

Printed in Canada
052016/WB20160328

**Library and Archives Canada
Cataloguing in Publication**

Durant, Alan, 1958-
    Little Bo-Peep's missing sheep / Alan Durant
; illustrated by Leah-Ellen Heming.

(Tadpoles: nursery crimes)
Issued also in electronic format.
ISBN 978-0-7787-8029-8 (bound).
--ISBN 978-0-7787-8040-3 (pbk.)

        I. Heming, Leah-Ellen II. Title. III. Series:
Tadpoles (St. Catharines, Ont.). Nursery crimes

PZ7.D9322Li 2012   j823'.914   C2012-904842-9

**Library of Congress
Cataloging-in-Publication Data**

Durant, Alan.
  Little Bo-Peep's missing sheep / written by
Alan Durant ; illustrated by Leah-Ellen Heming.
      p. cm. -- (Tadpoles: nursery crimes)
  Summary: When Little Bo-Peep's sheep go
missing one snowy morning, she is helped by
Mary, whose lamb is also missing, and other
familiar characters.
      ISBN 978-0-7787-8029-8 (reinforced library
binding : alk. paper) -- ISBN 978-0-7787-8040-3
(pbk. : alk. paper) -- ISBN 978-1-4271-9153-3
(electronic pdf : alk. paper) -- ISBN 978-1-4271-
9161-8 (electronic html : alk. paper)
      [1. Lost and found possessions--Fiction. 2.
Characters in literature--Fiction. 3. Mystery and
detective stories.] I. Heming, Leah-Ellen, ill. II.
Title.

  PZ7.D9317Lit 2012
  [E]--dc23
                                                        2012027819

Little Bo Peep's Missing Sheep

Written by Alan Durant
Illustrated by Leah-Ellen Heming

Crabtree Publishing Company

www.crabtreebooks.com

One snowy winter's morning, Little
Bo Peep looked out of her window—and
got a big shock. Her sheep were gone!

She picked up her crook and ran out into the meadow. No sheep! Where could they be? And where was her friend Little Boy Blue, who was supposed to be looking after them?

"Sheep, sheep!" she called.
"Little Boy Blue, where are you?"
Little Bo Peep was puzzled.

Then she saw hoofprints in the snow. "They'll lead me to my sheep," she thought. So, off she went following them.

Little Bo Peep hadn't gone very
far when she met Mary.
"Have you seen my sheep?"
asked Little Bo Peep.

Mary shook her head. "Have you seen my
little lamb?" she asked. "He was following
me to school, and when I looked around
he was gone. What am I going to do?"
she wailed.

Mary started to cry.
"There, there," soothed Bo Peep.
"We'll find him. He's probably with
my sheep. Come with me."

So Little Bo Peep and Mary
followed the trail of hoofprints
through the snow.

They went round and round a
mulberry bush, but there was no sign
of any sheep—just children pretending
to wash their hands.

"Have you seen my sheep?"
asked Little Bo Peep.
"And my lamb?" added Mary.

"No," said the children, "but this is the way we go to school, go to school, go to school," they sang. And off they went.

Little Bo Peep and Mary carried on following the hoofprints through the snow, until they came to the house that Jack built.

Little Bo Peep knocked. "Yes?" asked Jack.

"I've lost my sheep," said Little Bo Peep.
"And I've lost my lamb," added Mary.
"Have you seen them?" they asked.

"Come in and have a look," said Jack.
"It's my wedding party, you know."

It was very crowded in Jack's house.
There was a farmer with a bag of corn,
a crowing cock, a priest all shaven
and shorn, a maiden all forlorn,
a cow with a crumpled horn, and
a dog and a cat chasing a rat.

But no sheep. Yet, there, at the back
door, were the hoofprints again!

The hoofprints led to Mary's garden. "Oh, dear," said Little Bo Peep. Mary's garden was in a terrible state. There were silver bells and cockle shells all over the place.

"Look at my pretty maids," sighed Mary. "I planted them all in a row. What a mess they're in!"

At that moment they heard a noise.
Snip, snip, snip. It was coming from
behind the garden wall.

Snip, snip, snip.

Little Bo Peep and Mary went to investigate. "Oh, no!" they cried.

There was Tom, the piper's son, snipping the woolly coat of a sheep with a pair of scissors!

"Stop, thief!" Little Bo Peep commanded. "What are you doing to my sheep?" "I'm filling up these three bags with wool," said Tom. "One for the master, and one for the dame, and one for the little boy who lives down the lane."

He grinned. "That's me!"

"But you can't do that," wailed Little
Bo Peep. "Those sheep belong to me."
"And that little lamb belongs to me!"
added Mary.

Tom stuck out his tongue. "Prove it!"
he taunted.

Little Bo Peep and Mary looked
at each other. How could they prove the
sheep and the lamb belonged to them?

Suddenly...TAN-TARAN-TARA!
It was Little Boy Blue. He had just woken
up from his sleep under a haystack, and
he was blowing his horn!

At once the sheep turned and ran for home. The little lamb leaped up into Mary's arms.

"I think that proves it," said Little Bo Peep.

"Nuts!" said Tom with a scowl. "I would have gotten a good price for those sheep at the market."

"Excuse me," squealed a little voice. "Did you say market?" It was a small pig. "I'm on my way there, you see, but I'm rather lost."

Tom's scowl turned to a grin once more.
"I'll take you," he laughed, and he picked
up the pig and away he ran!

"That naughty boy," sighed Little Bo Peep.
"At least you got your sheep back," said Mary.

"And you got your little lamb,"
said Little Bo Peep.
"Baa," bleated the little lamb happily.

Then they followed the sheep home...
bringing this tale behind them!

Notes for adults

Tadpoles: Nursery Crimes are structured for transitional and early fluent readers. The books may also be used for read-alouds or shared reading with younger children.

Tadpoles: Nursery Crimes are intended for children who are familiar with nursery rhyme characters and themes, but can also be enjoyed by anyone. Each story can be compared with the traditional rhyme, or appreciated for its own unique twist.

IF YOU ARE READING THIS BOOK WITH A CHILD, HERE ARE A FEW SUGGESTIONS:

1. Make reading fun! Choose a time to read when you and the child are relaxed and have time to share the story.
2. Before reading, invite the child to preview the book. The child can read the title, look at the illustrations, skim through the text, and make predictions as to what will happen in the story. This activity stimulates curiosity and promotes critical thinking skills.
3. During reading, encourage the child to monitor his or her understanding by asking questions to draw conclusions, making connections, and using context clues to understand unfamiliar words.
4. After reading, ask the child to review his or her predictions. Were they correct? Discuss different parts of the story, including main characters, setting, main events, the problem and solution. Challenge the child to retell the story in his or her own words to enhance comprehension.
5. Give praise! Children learn best in a positive environment.

VISIT THE LIBRARY AND CHECK OUT THESE RELATED NURSERY RHYMES AND CHILDREN'S SONGS:

Little Bo Peep
Little Boy Blue
Mary Had a Little Lamb

Here We Go Round the
   Mulberry Bush
The House that Jack Built
Mary, Mary, Quite Contrary

Tom, Tom, the Piper's Son
Baa, Baa, Black Sheep
To Market, To Market

IF YOU ENJOYED THIS BOOK, WHY NOT TRY ANOTHER TADPOLES: NURSERY CRIMES STORY?

Humpty Dumpty's Great Fall	978-0-7787-8028-1 *RLB*	978-0-7787-8039-7 *PB*
Little Miss Muffet's Big Scare	978-0-7787-8030-4 *RLB*	978-0-7787-8041-0 *PB*
Mother Hubbard's Stolen Bone	978-0-7787-8031-1 *RLB*	978-0-7787-8042-7 *PB*

VISIT WWW.CRABTREEBOOKS.COM FOR OTHER CRABTREE BOOKS.